animals HOW?

HOW DO CROCODILES CLEAN THEIR TEETH?

Om KIDZ

An imprint of Om Books International

HOW?

CONTENTS

Find out!

Which is the smallest crocodile species in the world?

1 How do crocodiles clean their teeth?

Birds do the cleaning for the crocodile! After a heavy meal, a crocodile lies on the bank of a river or marsh with its mouth open. Birds, such as plovers, sandpipers and others, climb into the crocodile's mouth and pick the food stuck between its teeth. Birds use their sharp beaks to remove the bits of food from the crocodile's teeth. Isn't that amazing?

Pocket fact

Anacondas can hold their breath for up to 10 minutes when they are underwater. They also have eyes and nostrils that can pop out of the water's surface to increase their stealth and hunting power!

2 How are snakes able to swim without arms and legs?

Snakes swim by curving their bodies. They turn their bodies left, then right. You can observe them making a big 'S' as they swim. Each time they turn, they push the water behind them with their bodies, and move their bodies forward!

Find out!

Do ants have stomachs? If yes, what is the size of their stomach?

3 How many eyes do spiders have?

Two, four, six, eight and even 12! Most spiders have eight eyes that are on the top and front of their heads. The number of eyes depends on the type of spider. It is also interesting to know that web-spinning spiders have no eyes at all! But spiders have a very good sense of touch and smell which lets them experience the world around them.

Pocket fact

Patu marplesi is known to be the world's smallest spider. It is so small that you can fit 10 of them at the end of a pencil.

4 How big is an ant's brain?

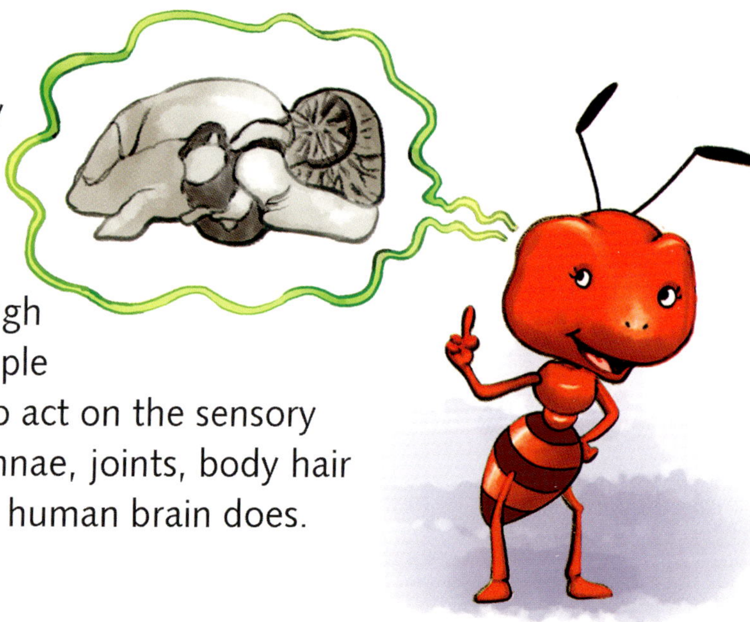

It's one-fourth the size of its body weight. The size of an ant varies from six to 20 millimetres. In that case, its brain size would range from 1.5 to five millimetres! Though small, an ant's brain can store simple information. This allows the ant to act on the sensory data that it receives from its antennae, joints, body hair and eyes. This is similar to what a human brain does.

5 How do ladybugs protect crops?

By eating insects! Besides being beautiful to look at, ladybugs are popular among farmers. Most ladybugs feed on plant-eating insects called aphids, and help protect the crops. They do so by laying hundreds of eggs in the colonies of aphids and other plant-eating insects. When they hatch, the ladybug larvae immediately begin to feed on these insects, upsetting the insect population, which in turn protects the crops from being destroyed.

6 How are wasps different from bees?

You can differentiate wasps from bees by their pointed lower abdomens and narrow 'waists', called a petiole. The petiole separates the abdomen from the thorax. Wasps are quite colourful, from yellow to bright red, whereas bees are golden yellow and black in colour. All wasps build nests using wood fibres, but bees secrete a waxy substance to build their hives.

Pocket fact

A wasp emits a pheromone in the air when it is attacked or is about to die. This acts as a warning signal to other wasps so that they become aware of the danger and come to rescue their friend.

Find out!

Where does the Arctic fox live in the winter season?

7 How do Arctic foxes hunt for their prey?

Arctic foxes have a unique and interesting style of hunting. They have wide, front-facing ears, which allow them to locate their prey beneath the snow. When an Arctic fox hears its prey under the snow, it leaps into the air and pounces on it. It breaks through the snow onto the prey beneath and has a tasty meal!

Pocket fact

A device called the 'wagometer' was invented by Dr Roger Mugford in 2003. It claims to interpret a dog's exact mood by measuring the wag of its tail.

8 How do dogs communicate?

Scent is their way! Dogs sniff each other's faces to communicate. A sniff can tell them how old a dog is, whether it's a male or female, familiar or a stranger. Scents also tell about a dog's confidence and his mood at the moment. Dogs collect all this information and understand very quickly what their relationship with another dog is likely to be!

Find out!

How can you identify a lion and a lioness?

9 How do cats see clearly at night?

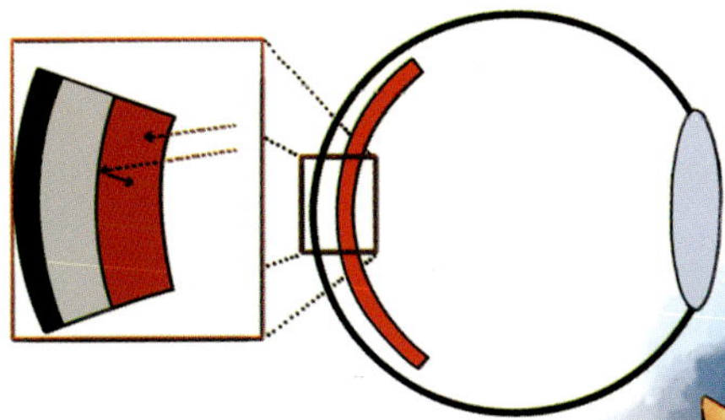

With the extra layer in their eyes! The eyes of a cat have an extra layer called the tapetum lucidum behind the retina. This layer reflects light back through the retina and enhances vision in low-level light. This allows cats to see clearly even when there is very dim or no light.

10 How are lions different from other members of the cat family?

Pocket fact

Himmy, a tabby from Queensland, Australia, is the heaviest cat known so far. It weighed nearly 21 kg and died at the age of 10.

Lions live in groups called 'prides'. Other cat species, like the tabby cat, live in solitude. A lion pride is a family unit that includes up to three males, a dozen females, and their young ones. All lionesses in a pride are related and unlike the males, stay with the group even after they grow up.

Find out!

Which bird lays the smallest eggs and which one lays the largest?

11

How do birds find their way south?

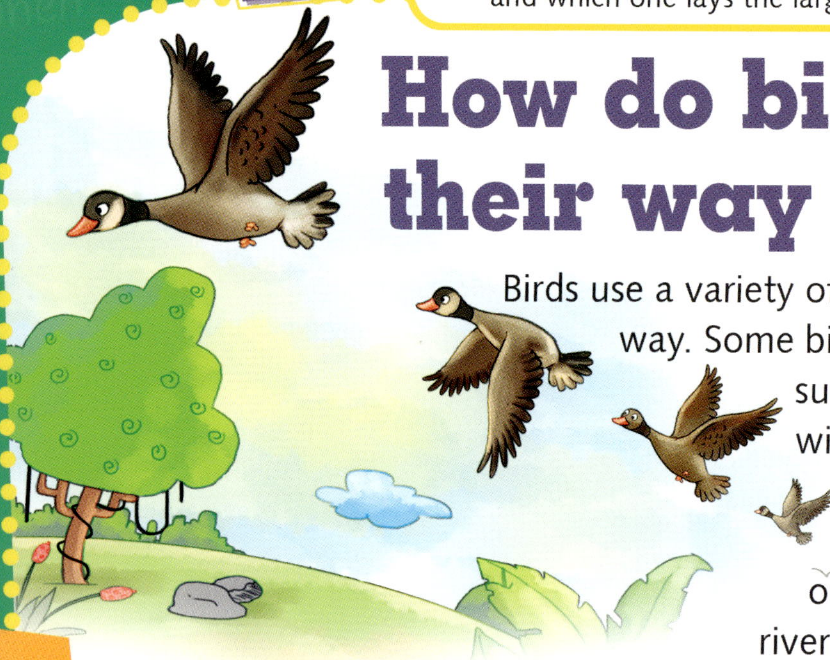

Birds use a variety of hints in order to find their way. Some birds use the position of the sun. Birds flying south for the winter, stay on track by using the sun's position in the sky as a guide. Some birds observe landmarks like lakes, rivers, or mountains, which help them know which way they are headed. Sometimes travelling south is as simple as following the path of a river that travels south to warmer temperatures!

Pocket fact

An ostrich never drinks water. This is because it produces water internally and also gets it from its food.

12

How do ostriches use their wings?

As rudders! Though flightless, ostriches are fleet, strong runners. They can sprint up to 70 kilometres an hour. Ostriches use their wings like the rudders of a boat to help them change direction while running. It's amazing to know that an ostrich can cover 10 to 16 feet in a single stride with its powerful, long legs.

Find out!

What is the similarity between a salamander and a frog?

13 How are mudpuppies different from puppies?

Mudpuppies are not puppies at all, but are salamanders that live at the bottom of lakes, ponds, rivers and streams. They never leave the water. Mudpuppies are also called waterdogs because their squeaky sounds are similar to a dog's bark.

14 How big can spotted salamanders grow?

Salamanders can grow up to nine inches! Spotted salamanders are members of the mole salamander family. They are named so because of the two rows of yellow and orange spots along their black back. On an average, spotted salamanders measure about seven inches in length, but some of them can grow up to nine inches.

Pocket fact

There are approximately 350 species of salamanders. Here are a few–
Hellbender: Has a thick body, a broad and flat head.
Amphiuma: Looks like a snake with tiny legs.
Siren: Resembles an eel with no hind legs.

Find out!

What were sea stars called earlier?

15 How are seahorses unique?

The male keeps the eggs in his pouch! Seahorses are truly unique because they are the only species on Earth in which the male bears the unborn young. Male seahorses have a pouch on their front side. The female seahorse deposits her eggs into the male's pouch, and he fertilises them internally. The male seahorse carries the eggs in his pouch until they hatch! When the baby seahorses grow, the father lets them go into the water.

Pocket fact

Seahorses do not have teeth or a stomach. The food they eat passes through their digestive systems so quickly, that they must eat almost constantly to stay alive!

16 How do sea stars grow their limbs again?

Sea stars are famous for their ability to grow their limbs again. They can do this because of a special type of connective tissue and response to nervous signals. This tissue is called catch connective tissue. Sea stars receive the right nervous signals from the rest of their body. This allows their cells to divide in such a way that they can regenerate new limbs.

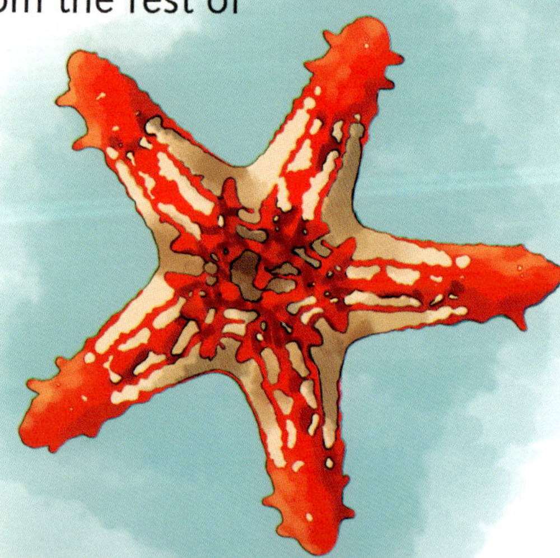

Find out!

Why do snails carry shells on their backs?

17 How do sharks hunt?

By sprinting and breaching! When sharks spot their prey at the surface of the water, they often position themselves underneath it. They swim upward at a fast sprint, and burst out of the water with a leap called a breach. They then fall back into the water with the prey in their mouths.

Pocket fact

The Carcharodon Megalodon was an ancient shark that had the largest teeth ever discovered. Its teeth were more than 6 inches long. Its jaws were so big that it could swallow an entire car, and it was the same length as the dinosaur T-Rex!

18 How is it that snails have antennae, but they are not insects?

Snails are not insects, but molluscs. Molluscs are animals with soft bodies. A snail has two pairs of antennae on its head. One pair is longer than the other and has eyes. The shorter antennae are used for smelling and sensing its way around. But, some species of snails have only one pair of antennae.

Find out!

What do rhinos do to keep themselves cool?

19 How are hippos different from other land mammals?

They are semi-aquatic! Hippopotami spend most of their time in lakes and rivers. Their eyes, ears, and nostrils are placed high on their skulls. This allows these organs to remain above the water's surface whereas the rest of the body is inside the water. When a hippo is underwater, its nose and ears automatically close so that no water seeps in. Unlike other land mammals, they have webbed feet that help them swim.

Pocket fact

The colour of a hippo's milk is bright pink. It is because a hippo secretes two kinds of unique acids called hipposudoric acid and norhipposudoric acid. These two acids together give its milk the pink colour!

20 How does a rhinoceros use its horns?

As weapons! Some rhinos have two horns, whereas some have just one. Their horns, which are on their nose, are made of a substance (keratin) that is also found in human fingernails. Rhinos with two horns use the bigger one as a weapon in fights. Female rhinos use their horns to protect their babies from predators such as lions, crocodiles, and hyenas.

Find out!

How do squirrels help new plants grow?

21 How do squirrels find the nuts they hide?

By smelling! Squirrels feed on nuts, seeds, buds, and flowers of trees. As winter approaches, squirrels collect nuts and other food, and bury them in several locations for later use. They are able to locate food that they have hidden using their excellent sense of smell. They can also pick up information about fellow squirrels by smelling them.

22 How are rabbits and hares different?

Rabbits and hares are not the same at all! Hares have longer ears and legs, whereas rabbits have shorter ears and legs. Hares don't live in burrows, while rabbits do. Baby hares are born with hair, but baby rabbits are born without hair!

Pocket fact

A rabbit named Darius is the world's largest rabbit. It weighs approximately 23 kilograms. It lives with its owner Annette Edwards in the UK. It has been reported that Darius thinks he is a dog!

Find out!

Can you name two diseases caused by mosquitoes?

23 How do mosquitoes choose their victims?

By detecting body chemicals! You are often irritated if a mosquito buzzes around you. Can you guess what attracts them? Human skin produces more than 340 chemical odours, and some of these attract mosquitoes. Mosquitoes are particularly fond of octenol, a chemical released in our sweat. They are also attracted by folic acid, certain bacteria, skin lotions, and certain perfumes.

Pocket fact

The legs of the first body segment of centipedes contain toxins, or poison. Centipedes use them to attack and capture their prey.

24 How many legs do centipedes have?

Not 100 as their name suggests! Centipedes belong to a class of insects that have their body divided into segments. Each segment has one pair of legs. Though the word 'centipede' means 100 legs, the number of legs in these creatures is between 15 and 171 pairs. Each species of centipede has a different number of legs. Interestingly, they always have an odd number of leg pairs.

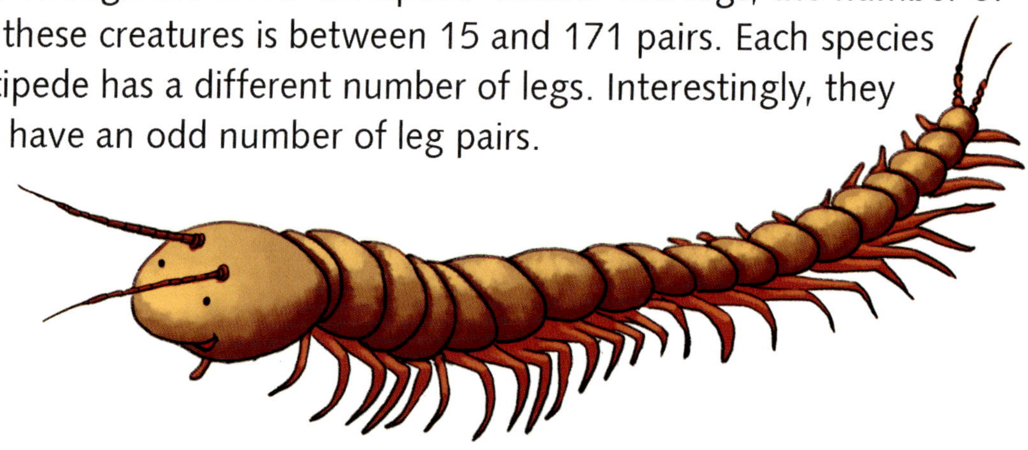

Find out!

Identify this worm and write its name.
Hint: The first part of its name is used to measure length.

25 How do worms move without legs?

Worms move using their muscles! Worms don't have legs, but have two kinds of muscles beneath their skin that make movement possible. The outer layer of muscles is circular and the inner layer of muscles is longitudinal. The segments of a worm's body (except the first and last) have four pairs of tiny, stiff hair-like projections called 'setae' that help it grip the soil and move.

Pocket fact

Worms do not have eyes but receptor cells. This helps them know that they are in, or too close to, light. They usually don't like light and die in the sunlight. They feel around with their sensitive skin and hair on their body.

26 How do earthworms make soil healthy?

By making tunnels, and some other tricks too! As earthworms move through soil, they make tunnels. Just like plowing a field, these tunnels allow air and water to get to the roots of the plants and help them grow. Earthworms eat dead leaves and grass. Their waste called 'castings' help enrich the soil because it's rich in phosphorus, calcium, nitrogen and magnesium. These are all important nutrients and make the soil healthy for plants to grow!

OTHER TITLES IN THIS SERIES